toddlers

Things I like best

by GERALDINE TAYLOR
illustrated by JULIE PARK

Where is your favourite place?

What do you like to wear?

Are your favourite

Helping at home.

What is your favourite job?

Come for a ride!

Which will you choose?

Things that fly.

Things to float.

Can you...

...wriggle like a worm?

...waddle like a duck?

buzz
...buzz like a bee?
buzz

gallop like a horse?

...h^op like a fr^og?

scamper like a mouse?

Favourite creatures.

his

mee-ow

croak

nibble

hiss

giggle   croak   woo

Do you like collecting things?

One day I'd like
to be...

Who would you most like to meet?

I'll huff and I'll puff and I'll blow their houses down!

Make a
special wish…

The land of favourite things.